In a land so inescapably and inhospitably cold,
hockey is the chance of life, and an affirmation that
despite the deathly chill of winter we are alive.

—STEPHEN LEACOCK

WHEN THE MOON COMES

Paul Harbridge

ILLUSTRATED BY

Matt James

tundra

WHEN
M
CO

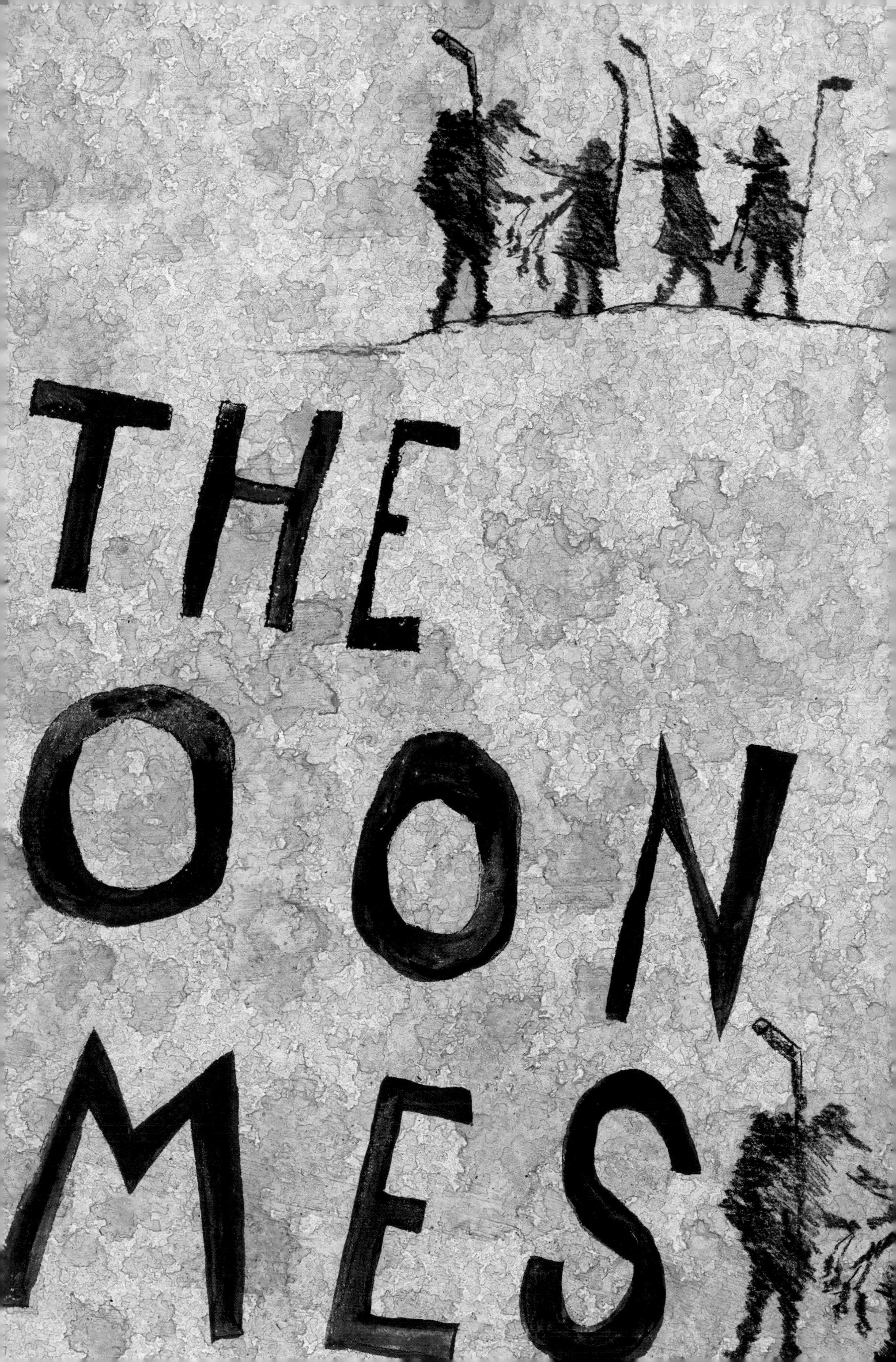
THE
OON
MES

November is mild. The ducks stay late on the big beaver flood in the woods behind Brunton's farm. There is no snow.

In December, before a single flake has fallen, the cold snap comes. For a week it is twenty below freezing, and when you walk in the woods, the leaves shatter under your feet like glass.

The beaver flood is ice now. The cold has come so fast that not a piece of snow or ripple of wind has frozen into the ice. It glistens smooth and perfect in the cold sun.

"Let's go now before we lose it," we say, but Arthur says, "No. We have to wait for the moon."

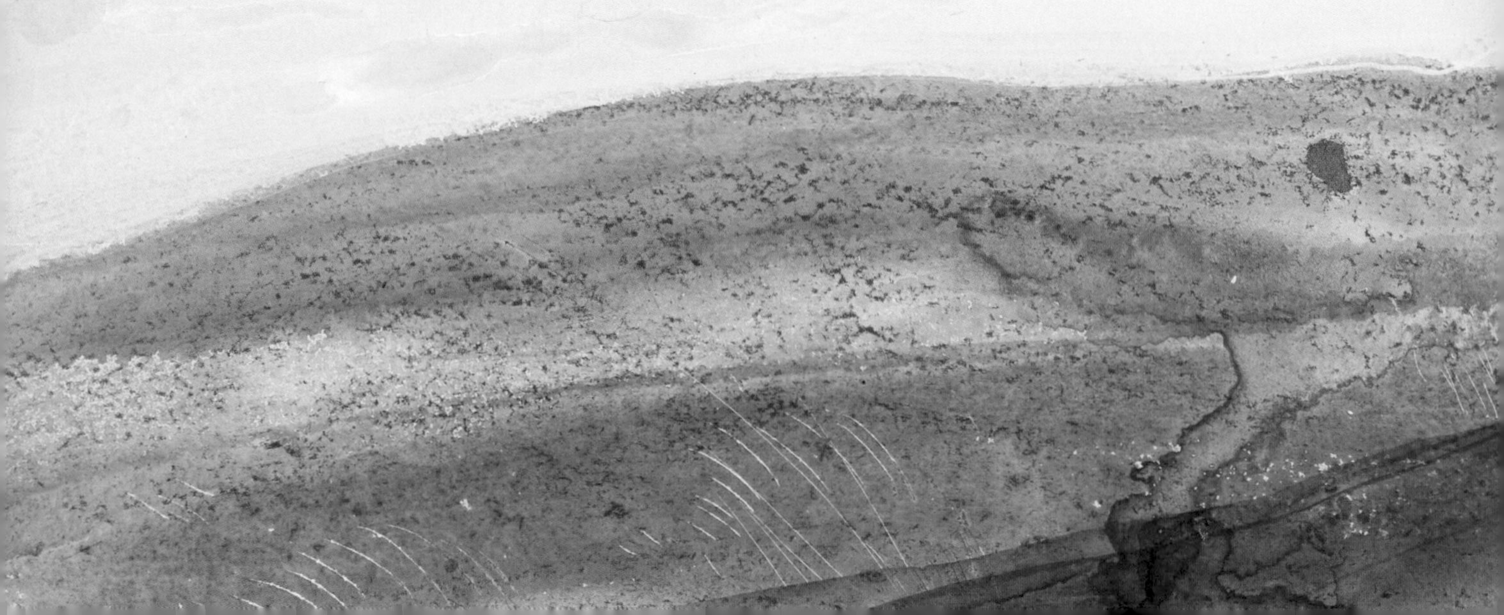

We see ducks in the sky, flock after flock,
sent south by the sudden cold.

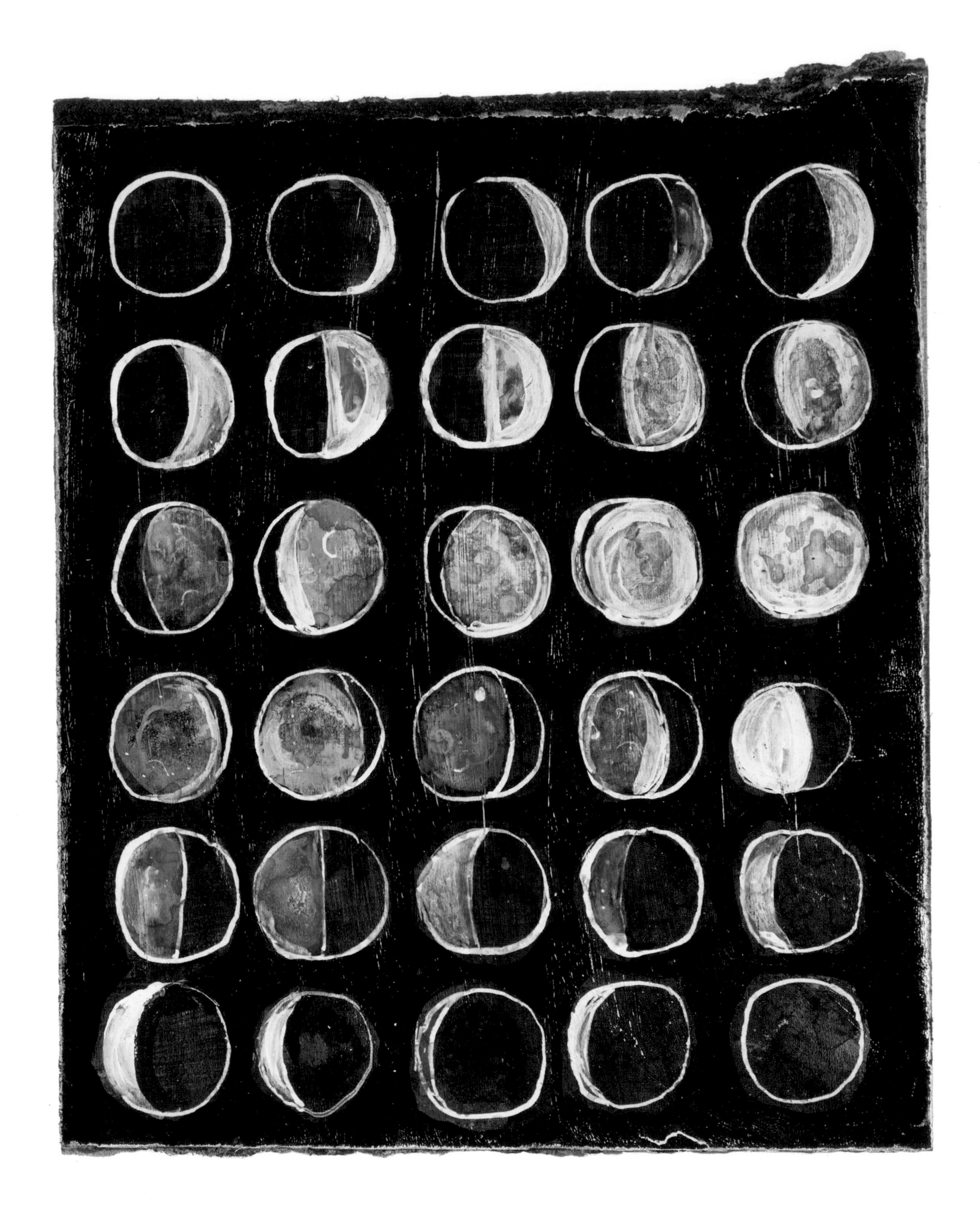

This week, the moon is growing.

Friday while we sleep, the snow comes. Half a foot when we wake up on Saturday, and it does not stop.

But Arthur says, “It’s okay. Our ice is waiting for us under the snow.”

Sunday night, we see the moon rise large and ready.

At Monday recess, we decide.
  "Tonight's the night." We pass the word. "Tonight's the night."

At four, we are on the road. The sun is almost down. Already the cold has settled, biting noses and cheeks.

At Mark's house, we send him back for his scarf and hat.

At Arthur's farm, we leave the road and wade into the logging trail, knee-deep in snow.

We walk between ridges, through dense tamarack swamp crisscrossed with rabbit tracks and up a high hill. In the distance we see the wide, snowy flat of the beaver flood.

Down the hill we stumble, and we are at the flood by dark. The snow has wet our pants, and our toes are cold at the end of our boots. We stamp and kick, and Arthur makes a fire.

The fire crackles high and hot. We sit on logs and
face our open skates to the flames, heating them
right to the toes. The harsh smoke burns all our
eyes in turn, but it is warm and we do not mind.

Out on the beaver flood, I feel through the snow with my stick, and Arthur is right. The ice is waiting, perfect.

"Wonderful ice," says Arthur. "Magic ice."

We take turns pushing the shovel, and it plows the light, playful snow as if there were nothing there at all.

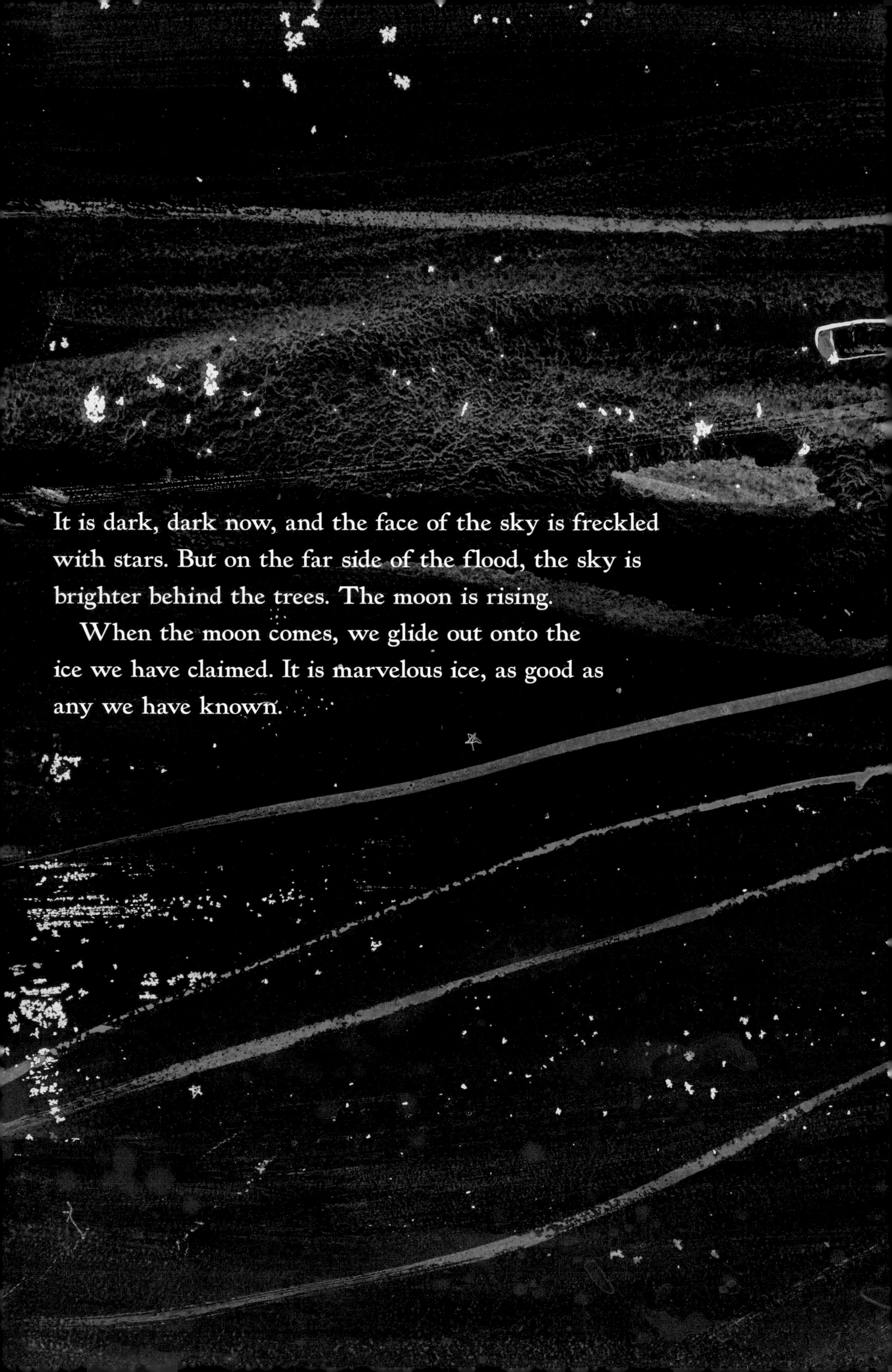

It is dark, dark now, and the face of the sky is freckled with stars. But on the far side of the flood, the sky is brighter behind the trees. The moon is rising.

When the moon comes, we glide out onto the ice we have claimed. It is marvelous ice, as good as any we have known.

The game is on, and our shouts rise up and disappear into the cold, black sky. End to end and around we fly, the long black stripes of our shadows moving across the moonlit ice.

We play hard and sweat, and the sweat freezes on hair and ears. We trip and fall into the snow, and it stings our cheeks as it melts, and the cold air burns our lungs.

We must be careful. It is so cold there is a ring around the moon.

I look far down the flood. I see something moving. A moose or a wolf or a bear. I look behind me into the shadows of the nearest trees and can see nothing but black.

Then Billy shoots too hard, and the puck flies underneath the powdery snow. Who knows how far down the flood it has sped?

"It's time," says Arthur. Tomorrow is school.

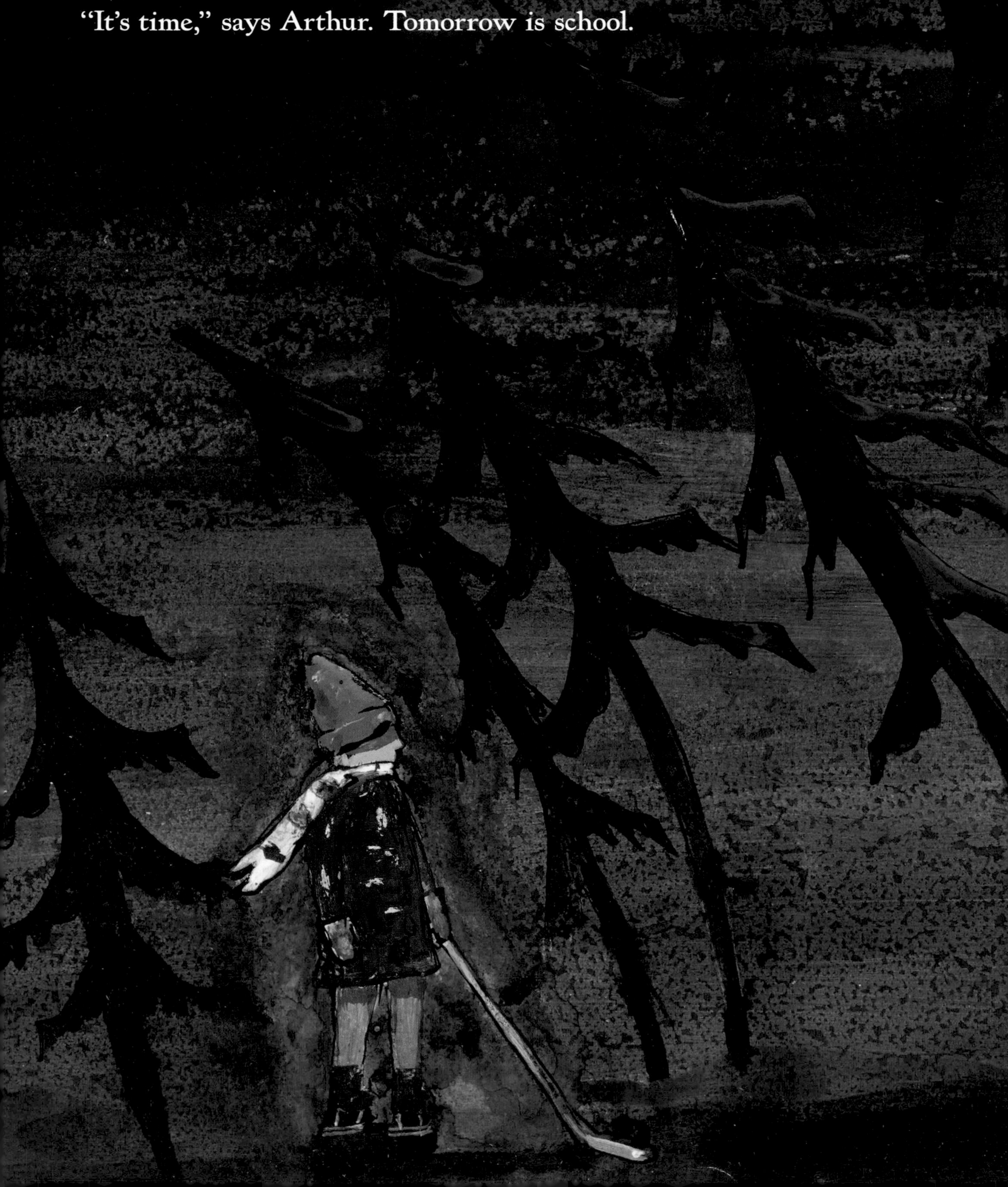

We skate puffing to the fire, and in a minute it burns high again. We fill a pot brimming with snow, and when it melts down, fill it again and again until it is full and boiling. We drink scalding tea and eat toasty sandwiches, then tramp contented back into the night.

At the top of the hill, we look back at the slash of silver lying silent now in the expanse of white, bordered all around by black forest.

Wonderful ice. Magic ice.

Back through the snow of the swamp we wade, the little blue shadows of rabbit tracks disappearing beneath our feet. Back between the ridges, keeping ever in the moonlight.

Our wet pants freeze solid in the cold, and we walk clanking like knights in armor, lances over our shoulders, hoods like helmets around our faces.

We reach the road and walk easy now, quiet and happy in the bright, bitter cold.

One by one we lose teammates to the warmth of their houses. Smoke rises from chimneys, moonlit white against the dark sky.

Then it is my turn and I am warm, deep under my blankets. But I cannot sleep.

The moon wants to pull me out the window and take me back. Back along snowy road and trail.

Back to that silent slash of silver in the cold, black night.